LITTLE
POLAR BEAR
RESCUE

Rachel Delahaye

LiTTLE TiGER
LONDON

For Ollie Callum who is wild about the natural
world, and a very big fan of polar bears
– Rachel

CONTENTS

Fun at the Campsite

"Who can tell us how to light a fire using things from the forest?" Karen, the Forest Club leader, looked around at the hands in the air. "How about you, Felicity?"

They were on a Forest Club camping trip in the woods and there was so much to see. Fliss was busy looking at a group of woodlice and hadn't heard the question.

"She wouldn't know how to start a

fire – she'd know how to start a zoo!"
Ella laughed.

"I want to be a vet, not a zookeeper!"
Fliss said. "They're completely
different!"

"That's very interesting, girls, but let's
get back to the topic of making a fire,"
Karen said. "Go ahead, Emile. Why
don't you tell us?"

"You can use cramp balls," he said.
"It's a fungus that grows on dead trees in
the shape of a black ball. If you break it
open, it's dusty inside and easy to light."

"Dusty black fungus balls!" Taylor
snorted. "Don't be silly!"

All the kids laughed and started
rolling around. Fliss didn't join in – she
didn't want to hurt Emile's feelings. But
it was hard not to see the funny side!

Karen and the other camp leader, Andrew, clapped their hands together for silence.

"Although it does sound far-fetched, Emile is actually right," said Andrew. "Cramp balls are great for helping to start a fire. They're also known as King Alfred's cakes or coal fungus. Well done, Emile."

Once everyone had calmed down they gave Emile a round of applause.

"So, next question. How do we arrange a fire so it has the best chance of staying alight?" Karen pointed to Pippa.

"Scrunch up some paper, then add a layer of kindling and arrange a cone of sticks and logs around that."

"Excellent answer," said Andrew.

"Now, who would like to show us their skills by lighting a *real* campfire? If it's successful we can celebrate with smores, also known as … melted marshmallows and chocolate biscuits!"

Everyone cheered. Ella got up and did a 'smores dance', which involved jumping around and shouting *more smores, more smores*.

"OK. But first let's build up an appetite with a big game of hide-and-seek." Andrew grinned. "Ella, seeing as you're on your feet and keen to take part, why don't you be the seeker?"

"I love seeking," Ella said, closing her eyes. "Ready, steady ... go! Twenty, nineteen, eighteen..."

There were shrieks of excitement as the children criss-crossed all over the place, looking for somewhere to hide. Emile lay flat on the ground in plain sight and Fliss nudged him with her foot.

"What are you doing, Emile?"

"I'm pretending to be a stick," he whispered. "You can be a stick too, if you like."

Fliss giggled. Emile always looked at life in an interesting way – he was one of a kind! She needed to find a hiding spot fast but she didn't fancy being a stick. She looked across at Ella, who was striking a new silly pose with every number she shouted out.

"Nine, eight, seven…"

Fliss didn't have long. Hoping Ella would be distracted by Emile's stick impression, she ran to her tent and snuggled deep down inside her sleeping bag. Just in time.

"Three, two, one! Ready or not, here I come!"

Fliss tried to stifle a giggle, expecting Ella to open her eyes and shriek "found you" at Emile. And when she didn't, Fliss thought maybe Emile's trick had worked! It wouldn't be the first time he had been right. Then came a yell.

"Found you!" Ella's voice was still loud, even though it was now in the distance. "Taylor, I said I saw you. You have to come out!"

The voices faded away and Fliss assumed Ella had gone further into the woods to look for the others. That gave her plenty of time to get out and find a better hiding place. But it was warm and comfortable in the sleeping bag... Although her heart was racing with the excitement of the game, Fliss found her eyes fluttering and then closing. It was so cosy!

BANG.

What was that? Fliss's eyes flew open. It sounded as if some kids had run past and thumped the tent. Fliss yawned. She must have fallen asleep!

She had no idea how long she'd been hiding. Perhaps everyone else had been found and they were all looking for her.

Fliss wriggled back up the sleeping bag and blinked. It was dark and the air was cold. Had she slept through the game, the campfire and dinner? There's no way Ella would have let her miss the smores! Feeling panicky, Fliss got out of the bag and stood up. The first thing she noticed was that her head wasn't touching the roof of the tent. Then she felt the floor beneath her feet – it was hard, like wooden boards, not soft, like a grassy campsite. What was going on?

Still unable to see clearly, Fliss stepped forwards with her arms outstretched until she reached a surface. It felt like a solid wall. Feeling along it she came to some stiff cloth – a blind. She pulled the blind and it rolled up. Light streamed in, so bright it hurt her eyes. She rubbed them and peered around, keeping her eyes half closed until they got used to the brightness.

Fliss was in a room. There were four bunk beds, each with a sleeping bag and blankets. She jumped as she heard another thud – not kids thumping a tent but wind buffeting against the building. Fliss pressed her nose against the window. Outside everything was white.

There was snow as far as the eye could see.

She wasn't in a campsite any more. It looked like she was in the middle of nowhere, at the end of the world.

The End of the World

Fliss left the bunk room and took a look around. It didn't take long! There were only three rooms in the whole hut. There was a sleeping area, a tiny bathroom and a living room with a kitchen at one end, an office at the other and an old sofa in the middle. A door from the living area led straight outside and Fliss wrenched it open to see if there was anything that could tell her where she was.

She stepped out and was hit by the

bracing weather. The sunshine was so pure it was like a camera flash, and the sharp wind rose and fell in sudden gusts. But the most astonishing thing was the cold – it was so cold that it made Fliss's teeth chatter. In front of her, the snowy ground gave way to a huge, flat sheet of ice. Had the sea frozen? Fliss could only take a few seconds of the freezing air before she shuffled back inside the hut and slammed the door shut.

"It's so cold, it could be the South Pole!" she said to herself. Not long ago she had found herself there, looking after the sweetest penguins.

She looked out of the window again at the expanse of white and wondered where on Earth she was and what animals could possibly be out there.

She knew there had to be at least one, because every other time she had ended up a long way from home it was for a reason – to rescue a baby animal that needed her help. But she couldn't help anything if she didn't warm up soon. The cold was getting into her bones.

There was a fireplace and Fliss spotted a log basket next to it with everything she needed. Remembering Pippa's instructions, she made a cone of small logs around some paper and kindling and held a match to it. Within minutes, the fire was roaring and Fliss rubbed the cold out of her skin. Now she could concentrate.

The room had two windows – one with a view of the frozen sea out front and another on the opposite wall. Through the second window, Fliss could see a range of snowy hills, and what was that? In the distance she could just about make out the flat slopes of roofs and a snow-ploughed road. It was a town! Good, so she wasn't completely alone. But she had to keep exploring until she found out where she was and what to do next.

The office part of the living room had a desk. On it was a computer and some books. Underneath, a pile of equipment was stashed in a large box. The walls were covered in pictures, charts and graphs. And a map! It had a small Canadian flag in the bottom corner and a curved dotted line at the top, which Fliss recognized as the Arctic Circle. So she was in the very north of Canada, right next to the North Pole –

no wonder it was so cold!

Fliss stared at the wiggly shape of coastlines. The sea was marked blue, and the land mostly white and empty. There were no big cities or landmarks, just a dot and the name Winston, which had to be the town she'd seen. And there was another tiny dot labelled 'LOOKOUT'. It was on the south side of a large, sweeping C-shaped bay.

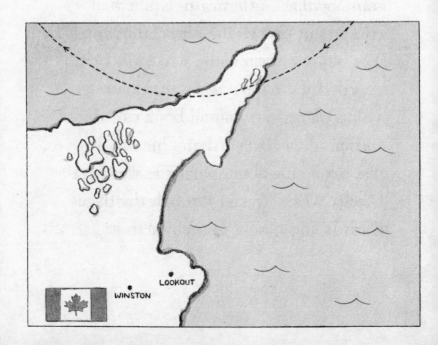

Fliss gazed out of the windows again. A bay straight ahead, with land behind and wide sea open to the right... That must be it! She was in remote Canada, in a lookout hut! But what was the hut a lookout for? Whales? Ships? No, surely it would be on the coast for those things. This was in a bay.

Her eyes travelled along the wall to a large, handwritten sheet with the title: *Polar Sightings – Threat Levels.* She had worked out that she was near the North Pole but she wasn't sure what was being recorded. Perhaps it was the sea level.

Fliss picked up a small book called *Animals of the Arctic*. Aha! This might give her a clue about what she was here to help... She flicked through the pages of birds and beasts. It seemed that quite a few animals lived in or near the Arctic Circle! Looking up, she again saw the town in the distance. Perhaps she should walk into Winston and speak to the local people. They might know of a distressed animal or at least where to look for one.

Then something outside the back window caught Fliss's eye, between the hut and the distant town. A large white shape was moving on a snow mound. Maybe it was a ball of snow, rolling down the hill? Those gusts of wind could be fierce. Surely they weren't fierce enough to blow away a chunk of snow *that* big. The lump continued to move, and there was another one behind it.

Fliss rummaged in the box under the desk and found a pair of binoculars.

Perfect! She took them to the window, put them to her eyes and adjusted the focus until the snow mound came into view, crystal-clear.

Now she could see them, the white fur, the black noses... It was a polar bear and her cub!

3

The Lookout

Fliss took another look at the Polar
Sightings sheet on the wall. It wasn't
polar as in North Pole. It was polar
as in polar bears! If she'd looked at
it more closely before she might have
worked it out. There were several
entries:

*Three mothers seen leaving den with cubs
in direction of town. Alerted Winston.
3rd March.*

Mothers headed out to ice. 5th March.

Two males spotted heading towards town.
Alerted Winston. 6th March.

So this was a polar bear lookout.
Fliss knew that hungry bears could
attack humans. Whoever was doing
shifts in the lookout had to warn the
town if bears were coming their way.
It was quite a responsibility!

There was a walkie-talkie on the desk
and Fliss wondered if she should use
it to let the town know about the polar
bears she'd spotted. But if they weren't
heading towards town – she didn't want
to create a fuss. She decided to check
they were going in that direction before
doing anything hasty.

Fliss returned to the window with the binoculars. The mother bear was still making her way down the snow hill towards the hut. She wasn't like the polar bears Fliss had seen in books or on documentaries. Those were big fluff balls and this one was scrawny. Her fur looked like a yellowy shaggy carpet and she was thin and malnourished.

You must be hungry after a winter in your den raising cubs, Fliss thought.

The little bundle tumbled after its mother and Fliss smiled. It looked as though it was the first time it had ever seen snow. It probably was!

The cub was chunky and healthy-looking. His mother's milk must have kept him well fed during the winter months. The young bear tried to leap

on its mother's back but the big bear
didn't stop walking.

"Hey, little one, your mum needs
some food!" Fliss laughed.

The mother bear had clearly had
enough! She lay on her tummy and
slid all the way down the hill. The
cub tried to run after her but fell
and skidded too. It was like a snowy

helter-skelter! The young bear landed
in a heap at the bottom. It rolled
around before chasing after its mum,
who was now walking past the hut.
Fliss ran to the other side of the room
and looked through the front window.
The bears were heading for the sea
ice! There was no need to alert the
people of Winston.

As she watched the beautiful bear family padding off into the distance, Fliss wished there was a way of getting closer. She knew that wasn't possible though – there was a reason they had lookout huts. Adult bears could be vicious, especially if they were hungry or looking after cubs. This mother bear was both of those things! She might have been thin but she was still so big a human wouldn't stand a chance if she decided to attack.

Then the polar bears were gone. Fliss put down the binoculars, her heart beating fast. She felt so lucky to have seen them.

Why am I here? she thought again. *If it's not for the polar bears, then what?*

Fliss flicked through the *Animals of the Arctic* book. There were magnificent reindeer called caribou, Arctic foxes, snow hares… With the bears safely out on the sea ice, she could now go and investigate. An animal might be stuck. She had to check the area.

Searching through the box for whatever else she might need, Fliss found a backpack with *Arctic Survival* written on it. A survival kit would definitely come in handy! She also found boots, gloves and snow goggles, and on the back of the door were salopettes. They were a bit big so she rolled up the legs and tightened the braces over her shoulders. She slipped a jacket over the top and was ready to go, with the animal book in her pocket and the binoculars round her neck.

One last look at the information sheets

on the wall told her that it was March 14th and sunset was at 5.20 p.m. A clock on the wall said 10 a.m. She had plenty of daylight left to rescue a baby animal!

Fliss stepped outside the hut. Only then did she see that it was covered in spikes. She gulped. They must be there to protect the person inside from hungry bears… A lone human in a little hut would be an easy snack.

Fliss didn't feel entirely safe leaving the shelter but she knew that somewhere out there an animal was in trouble. If she didn't get to it in time, she would never forgive herself. And what would happen to *her*? If this was like every other time that she had found herself transported to a distant land, only a successful rescue would send her back home.

A sudden scraping noise made her
jump. A chunk of snow had fallen
off the roof! Fliss laughed at how
nervous she was and took a deep breath,
enjoying the cold, clean air. Which way
should she go – straight ahead to the sea
ice or towards the town?

She walked to the edge of hut and
turned to look at the town. The view

of Winston was blocked by the snow hill – the one the mother and cubs had tumbled down. Now she could see something white on top of it. Was it a snow hare?

Fliss lifted the binoculars to her eyes to get a better look.

No. It was a bear cub. Another polar bear cub!

4

One Little Cub

At the top of the snow hill Fliss could
see that the cub was sitting alone.

I don't understand, she thought. *The
mother and her cub have gone. Unless…*

"Oh no! You got left behind!"

The cub didn't seem to know what
to do with itself so Fliss approached
carefully, keeping an eye out in case the
mother bear realized that she'd forgotten
one of her children. Slowly she made
her way up to where the little cub was

sitting, patting at the snow.

"Hello, you," Fliss said softly as she got closer.

The cub sprang to its feet and ran at her. It was the size of a small dog with extra big paws. Fliss thought it would stop, but it didn't. Filled with excitement, the cub tumbled towards her and crashed into her legs, knocking Fliss over in the deep snow. Then it sat back and stared at her curiously. Fliss laughed loudly and the bear jolted in shock at the sound, making her laugh even harder.

When she got her breath back, Fliss stood up and dusted off the snow. "If you're that keen to be friendly then we'd better introduce ourselves right away. I'm Fliss!"

The cub continued to look at her so Fliss kept talking. "You have a beautiful home!" she said, sweeping her arm at the view.

From the top of the hill she could see everything. On one side there was Winston, on the other was the bay. The wide sea was beyond that, covered in ice. She also noticed, now that some of the snow had slid off, the words *Nanuk Lookout* on top of the hut.

"Nanuk – that's a nice name," she said, smiling down at the cub. "How about we call you that?"

Fliss knelt back down in the snow to
get a better look at Nanuk. As the cub
rolled around she could see it was a boy.
He had cute little semicircle ears, dark
eyes and a black nose. He looked like a
beautiful wintery teddy bear and she
desperately wanted to cuddle him. But
she knew from her nature documentaries
that touching a wild animal wasn't wise.
It was always better to observe.

Nanuk, however, had other ideas.
He jumped into Fliss's lap and tried
to lick her hand with his little pink
tongue. Fliss still didn't give him a
cuddle. Instead she stayed still and
let him climb all over her. Then Nanuk
sat down, apparently delighted by a bit
of snow. He patted it until it formed a
snowball and held it between his paws.

While the cub was busy, Fliss thought it would be a good time to look in the animal book and find out as much as she could about polar bear cubs. If she was going to be responsible for Nanuk then she had to be armed with knowledge. She read aloud so Nanuk got used to her voice.

"Pregnant mothers eat as much as they can in summer and nothing during the winter. They build dens in mounds of soft snow, where they give birth to their cubs. They don't come out until the cubs are around four months old."

There was a picture of a mother and her two cubs emerging from a den. Fliss noticed how thin Nanuk's mother was compared to the one in the book. *Why was that?* she wondered.

"I think we should follow your mum, Nanuk. If she sees you, I'm sure she'll take you back. Although I can't work out why she would leave you in the first place. You're chunky enough to survive the cold and lively enough to keep up with her. Which way did she go?"

Fliss thought a moment and looked around. Then it came to her – follow the footprints, of course! She could see

big oval pads, and little ones, nearby.
Fliss and her friends had identified
animals by their prints at Forest Camp
that morning. She wondered briefly
how everyone was getting on and if
they'd eaten the smores yet. She smiled
sadly as she imagined Ella with sticky
marshmallow all over her face, singing a
campfire song...

Fliss looked at her very own
marshmallow bear. "Come on, Nanuk.
Let's check out these prints in the snow.
I think they belong to your mother and
brother or sister. Look! You can see
where they slid down. That's definitely
them. But what's this?"

Halfway down the slope Fliss spotted
a large hole. She looked closer and saw
that a tunnel had been hollowed out,

leading deep into the snow hill. Nanuk
stopped alongside her and peered in too.

"Was this your den?" Fliss said,
seeing how the little bear sniffed the
entrance. He then sniffed the snow in
front of the den opening and shrunk
back, afraid. Fliss noticed that dotted
around the area were more imprints.
They were different sizes and all shaped
like dog paws. Surely there wasn't
a pack of dogs living in such cold
conditions?

Wait a minute! Fliss had an idea and
flicked through her animal book. There
it was – the northern grey wolf, known
to attack small animals and bear cubs
for food. If wolves had arrived on the
scene, then Nanuk wouldn't have been
able to leave the den. And meanwhile,

his mum and the other cub had continued their journey.

"She didn't leave you on purpose. You got separated!" Fliss cried.

Nanuk danced around her feet, and Fliss suddenly thought of the energy he must be using up. "You still need your mother's milk, and there's no more of that until we find her. Let's go."

Before Fliss followed the bears' paw prints towards the coast, she took another look at the roofs of Winston in the distance. It was reassuring to know there were other people in the area. With them and the survival kit she would have help if she got into trouble. Though she hoped it wouldn't come to that.

Following Paw Prints

The slide marks went all the way down the hillside. The paw prints continued at the bottom and Fliss set off in their direction, assuming Nanuk would follow. But when she stopped for a moment to look at the frozen bay ahead, there was no crunch or brush of paws on the snow. She turned round and saw the cub had stopped to play with yet another snowball.

"Nanuk!" she shouted, her voice

travelling easily on the clear air.

The bear looked up and, realizing it had fallen behind, broke into a run. It was the sweetest run Fliss had ever seen – more a scoot than a run. He padded forwards on his big front paws and then pulled the back two behind in one movement.

They got to a ridge with a gradual slope on the other side that went right down to the rocky shore. It wasn't as steep as the hillside and it was a lot longer. Fliss couldn't face walking down in the thick snow. Nanuk was still frolicking like a new lamb that had just stood for the first time. Fliss wished she could be so light on her feet. It was hard work, moving in deep snow.

"Don't waste your energy, little

bear!" Fliss said. "We could have a long journey ahead. I've got an idea… Actually, it was your mother's idea. Now, do what I do."

Fliss lay on her back and pushed herself down the slope. At first it was slow, then she started slipping faster. She raised her head and looked behind. Nanuk was following on his tummy and they slid down together, Fliss laughing at the blue sky above her. She was tobogganing with a polar bear!

When they reached the bottom of the slope, Nanuk sprang on to Fliss's tummy and began to pat at her face with his giant padded paws. Fliss spluttered as he smudged snow across her nose. Silly Nanuk!

Before she realized what she was doing, Fliss had wrapped her arms round him in a big cuddle. Nanuk didn't seem to mind and Fliss enjoyed the soft, fuzzy feel of his fur. She was enjoying it so much she almost forgot her mission – to find his mum!

"There's no time for games, Nanuk. We need to keep following the trail."

They walked the remaining distance to the shore, where the paw prints stopped and rock and stones started to peek out from beneath the slow-melting snow.

In front of them was the icy bay. Fliss spotted a jetty, not far from the hut, where several medium-sized boats had frozen in their moorings. Straight ahead Fliss could see land on the north side of the bay. On the ice in between there were no bears to be seen. Looking to her right, where the bay opened out into the sea, Fliss could make out the shapes of some distant islands. There was nothing between here and there but a pile of lumpy rocks.

"Polar bears only eat seals and I'm guessing the seals are way out there! But I can't see your mum anywhere! Where did she go?"

Fliss looked through the binoculars and scanned every inch of the horizon. There were no bear shapes to be seen from here.

They could make their way across the frozen bay towards the open sea, but walking on ice was going to be very hard indeed. And was there any point if they weren't sure Nanuk's mother was there?

"I'll think of something," Fliss said decisively. "In the meantime, let's check the land on the other side of the bay. There might be a better view up the coast. And we should have a quick look in those boats too. There might be some food or other things that could help me with all this snow! Walking poles or snowshoes would be good!"

Without thinking about how the surface had changed, Fliss stepped forwards on to the sea ice and immediately slipped, landing on her bottom.

"Ow! That was a bad start. I'm better on the ice than you think, Nanuk! I was taught to walk on it by a penguin – I'll show you."

Fliss managed to get to her feet and started to waddle like a penguin, with her weight always on the front foot. Nanuk skated past her gracefully on his big flat paws.

"How do you do that?" Fliss laughed. "OK, you win!"

Fliss waddled carefully to a boat, happy to be able to hold on to something. She leaned over and looked in the storage box. There wasn't a lot there, just some fishing net. Who knew when fishing net could come in useful? She folded it into her backpack shuffled along to the next boat. It was a little newer and better equipped – it even had a rescue kit containing a box with a flare inside it. Perfect!

Fliss had done an advanced survival course with Forest Club and knew how to use one. It'd be handy if she got lost and needed to signal for help. She took the flare and put it carefully in her backpack, along with the fishing net. It was probably time to get going, although she still didn't know where she should go. Perhaps if they could reach the other side of the bay she might be able to see more clearly.

"No more slip-sliding, Nanuk," Fliss said, watching her friend cruise across the ice on his tummy. "We need to go."

Fliss was looking down at her feet, checking her waddle stance when she heard a huge belch.

"Nanuk!" She glanced at the little bear. He had a cheeky look on his face. She couldn't believe such a small creature could make such a big noise!

Fliss continued her waddle back towards the shore but stopped as her ears were met by a flurry of angry bellows, growls and snorts.

Those were definitely not noises you'd hear from a bear cub.

6

Big and Blubbery

Fliss narrowed her eyes as she looked in the direction of the noise. It was coming from further out in the bay.

"I thought they were rocks!" Fliss exclaimed, as the large brown lumps started moving.

Of course they weren't rocks. What would rocks be doing out there! The belching, bellowing lumps were awkwardly heaving themselves forwards. Fliss steadied herself on the ice and

looked through her binoculars to be
sure.

The creatures were big and heavy,
with huge tusks. Walruses! Fliss looked
again. She spied smaller walrus calves
in the big huddle. If they had babies
then the adults would be protective...
They could be angry! Fliss gasped as
she saw six giant walruses coming her
way, approaching faster than she could
run. On ice she couldn't run at all. She
was trapped...

"Oh no, we're going to get crushed!"
she gasped.

The walruses bellowed and pounded
the ice with their enormous bodies.
They were so close now Fliss could see
exactly how big they were. As tall as a
grown man and just as wide, with huge

long bodies stretching out behind them. It looked as if they weighed a ton.

Sensing danger, Nanuk skidded to Fliss's side. Fliss was terrified. She had to think fast.

If she tried to run, she'd fall over on the ice. But if they could slide on the ice to the other side of the bay, they might just move faster than the walruses and be safe.

"Watch, Nanuk! This is another thing I learned from a penguin."

Fliss launched herself on to her tummy and Nanuk skidded alongside her. Together they glided parallel to the shoreline. Behind them the walruses had slowed down. They obviously didn't think Fliss was a threat at this distance. She stopped and watched them wobble back to their group like big shuddering chocolate jellies. Usually she would have laughed at the sight, but her own tummy was quivering with fear and her heart was racing. She'd never expected to be so close to such enormous tusks!

"We may as well keep going like this," Fliss said, spinning herself on the ice on her bottom. "It's fun!"

Nanuk and Fliss skidded and skated

across the ice to the shore on the other
side of the bay. There, the landscape was
hillier – and higher ground would give
Fliss a better lookout. She glanced back
at the way they'd come. The hut was no
longer visible and Fliss could barely see
the great honking walruses out on the ice.

"I can't believe I thought that sound
was you!" She laughed, looking at
little Nanuk. "And it's made me realize
something. This isn't my environment
and I'm going to be slower than every
animal we might meet. I'm worried I
can't protect you."

Nanuk leaped on to the shore and
sniffed at a pile of debris.

"What's that?" Fliss said, skipping
towards him. She was much happier
to be on a surface that wasn't quite

so slippery. She wasn't looking forward
to walking in deep snow again, though,
where every step was an effort.

The debris was the remains of an old
wooden boat that had been washed up
before the freeze. Only a few curved
planks and beams and shards of wood
were left, tangled in fishing line. It
reminded Fliss of the Forest Club
session where they'd bound sticks
together to create fences or roofs for
dens. She should use those skills to
help her now! Maybe she could build a
small sledge, although that would only
be helpful going downhill. And she had
mastered sliding for that problem!

Or how about snowshoes? she thought,
her eyes widening. She looked at Nanuk,
who had wandered up a small bank of

snow. His four oversized paws were on top of the snow, hardly pressing down into it. Whenever she stepped in snow her two feet always sank down.

"The reason I sink into the snow is because all my weight is on two small feet. If I can spread the weight I won't sink so deep. That's it, Nanuk!"

Fliss returned to the old boat and pulled out two long thin wooden boards. She placed them on the ground in front of her and stood with a foot on each. Now she had to attach them. There was fishing line but only enough to tie on one of the boards. What else could she use? Then she remembered – the netting from the fishing boat!

Using the netting to keep the other board in place, Fliss stepped forwards on her two makeshift snowshoes. "Now to test them out."

She moved towards Nanuk, lifting each foot high before placing it down. Instead of her feet disappearing into the deep snowdrift, they just broke the top layer and Fliss was able to move without so much strain on her thigh muscles.

"Come on, Nanuk. I'm ready to go! Let's get up the next hill and see what we can see. Who knows, your mum might be over the other side."

With her wooden boards Fliss trudged much more easily up the hill and Nanuk ran alongside her, trying to chew at the netting and string. When they got to the top, Fliss forgot to stop and dig her shoes into the snow. There was no time to look for bears as she slipped over the top of the mound and slid down the other side. They were no longer snowshoes but more like skis, and she was getting faster and faster.

"Nanuk! Help me!" she half laughed, half screamed. The cub ran and tumbled down the slope with her, thinking it was a game, until Fliss hit a bump at the bottom and flew forwards, landing face first in the snow.

As she scraped the snow off her
face, Fliss heard a strange noise. From
Nanuk's rigid and scared posture,
she knew he was making the sound.
Something was wrong.

Fliss looked up. Directly ahead,
a pack of enormous wolves were
blocking the path.

The Pack

Fliss counted seven wolves in total. They were just a few metres away. They stood perfectly still, each with one leg slightly forwards as if ready to spring.

They were beautiful creatures, lean and strong. In other circumstances, she would have loved to admire their gleaming grey and cream coats, and the markings round their eyes that fanned out to frame their faces. But right now she knew she had to protect Nanuk.

The little cub backed against her legs in fear. Fliss stood over him, a foot on each side of his quivering body, wondering how he knew to be scared of wolves.

Fliss remembered the paw prints outside the polar bear den. These were probably the wolves that had disturbed Nanuk as he was trying to get out after his mother and sibling had gone. Their sense of smell was incredibly powerful and they probably had his scent in their noses. Perhaps they had even sniffed him out and followed him to the other side of the bay. They were here for the cub.

Even though she knew it was part of the cycle of nature, the thought shocked her. Fliss looked up into the eyes of the huge dog at the front of the pack. They were a cool pale amber colour and they stared right back. Their ears were pricked, occasionally turning to locate a distant sound. The wolves at the back moved side to side, occasionally whining. The front one didn't move an inch. It was as if it was waiting for her to leave Nanuk unprotected so it could attack.

From past experiences with animals, Fliss had learned that most creatures tried to look bigger when in danger. Fliss stood on tiptoe and held out her arms. The wolves weren't fooled and they'd had enough of waiting. They edged closer, placing each paw down carefully as if they were on a tightrope. There was something chilling about their precision and Fliss knew that when they decided to attack it would be so quick she'd hardly have time to think.

She also knew that when they did attack, there would be no way she could protect herself and Nanuk from seven gnashing sets of teeth… She felt her heart bang against her ribcage with fear. If only she had something that would scare *them*.

She thought fast through the options. She could throw her snowshoes, although if she bent down to untie them she would be unbalanced. She would also be exposing Nanuk… That wouldn't do. A shoe wouldn't hold them back for long, anyway. What else was there?

Fliss remembered the survival kit in her backpack and shrugged it round to her front. She didn't want to crouch down, as it would make her look small, so she pulled it up to her chest and stuck her hand inside. She felt around and found a whistle. There was also something hard and bulky – what was it? The flare she had taken from the boat!

Bright lights and noise. It was worth a shot.

With the whistle in her mouth and the flare gun pointing upwards, Fliss shot the flare and peeped as loudly as she could. The red flare roared into the sky like a rocket firework, hissing and spluttering. She blew hard on the whistle,

knowing that dogs' hearing was more sensitive to noises that were high-pitched.

The wolf pack retreated immediately, then ran away. Fliss saw them sprint until they were a safe distance away, then slow to a trot. They looked back at Fliss and Nanuk but must have decided it wasn't worth the trouble. As the wolves continued on their way, Fliss flopped to the ground with exhaustion.

"Are you OK, Nanuk?"

The little bear, also shocked by the flare, had fallen over backwards. Fliss pulled him towards her and gave him a hug.

"It's all right," she soothed. "I'm not going to let a wolf or anything else hurt you."

Fliss was shaken. They had survived their encounter with the wolves this time but a small cub was easy prey. What would she do if anything like that happened again? She didn't have any more flares.

No more ice-skating or skiing or making snowballs. She had to get him to the safety of his mother, right away. But where was she?

Fliss opened the animal book again, looking for any useful information. Nanuk had recovered quickly from the shock and started to play at her feet. He wrapped his paws round her calves as if he were a brown bear trying to climb a tree. Then he tugged at her trousers, trying to pull her to the ground.

"I'm trying to become a polar bear expert in a very short time," Fliss scolded. "And you're not helping!"

As if he'd been properly told off, Nanuk backed away, his head hanging low.

"Are you upset that I told you off? Come here, silly, I was only teasing."

The cub had started swaying his head from side to side.

"You're acting very strangely. Are you pretending to be a wolf? Let's see." In the book, Fliss found a list of polar bear behaviours. "It looks like you're either about to attack me or you want to play. Which one is it?"

Fliss wasn't scared. If Nanuk had gone wild, he was small enough to push away. She braced herself for the impact as he started to charge.

Quick as a Fox

Nanuk raced forwards in his galloping shuffle, leaping at the last minute and thwacking Fliss in the tummy. The impact knocked the book right out of her hands and she toppled sideways, landing with her face in the snow. She was getting used to that!

Now to see if that was the cub's attempt at an attack... Fliss rolled over and lay there as Nanuk inspected the damage he'd done. Then he jumped on her chest and started to lick her chin.

"I guess that means you just wanted to play!" Fliss laughed. "Or is it your way of saying sorry?"

It was hard to talk with a polar bear licking your face so Fliss sat up and gathered the fluffy bundle in her arms. *I shouldn't be doing this,* she thought. But it was Nanuk who kept making contact with her. If she was keeping his spirits up until he was back with his mum then perhaps it was a good thing.

Fliss couldn't help worrying about his mum – somewhere out there, missing her baby. She wondered how the bear would react if she saw Fliss cuddling her cub… A protective mother was a force to be reckoned with.

Fliss briefly pictured her own mum before pushing the thought aside. She needed to rescue this bear before she could get back home.

"Let's be serious, little one," Fliss said, pushing Nanuk gently from her lap. "From here we can see the sea beyond the bay. Your mother might be out there, searching for seals."

Looking through the binoculars, however, Fliss couldn't see anything. She scanned the area slowly and thoroughly, looking for the yellowy tinge of the mother polar bear's coat. She could only see ice. Miles and miles of grey-white ice.

"This is strange. Your mum was hungry, I know it. So why isn't she out there hunting?"

If she wasn't at sea then maybe she'd followed the scent of something inland. Bears had obviously gone into the town in the past – that's why there was the Nanuk Lookout and its warning system. What if Nanuk's mother had headed to Winston? Fliss's heart skipped a beat. No one would have warned the townspeople! If the polar bear got too close to the humans, someone – a bear or a person – might get hurt.

"Nanuk, we have to go into town," Fliss said. "We'll walk back to the other side of the bay where the hut is but that's going to take ages. We need to hurry."

While they had been playing, a low yellow cloud had covered the blue sky and it had started to snow. It made it much more difficult to work out exactly where she was. Blinking against the swirling snow, Fliss couldn't see anything that would help guide her. She closed her eyes and thought of the times she and her Forest Club had orienteered in the woods, using only a compass. A compass... Of course! There would be one in her survival kit. Sure enough, it was tucked inside one of the pockets. Now she just needed to work out which direction to head in.

Fliss closed her eyes and pictured the

map on the wall back at the hut. She
was north of the bay and the hut was
south of the bay. The town was maybe
a mile inland from the hut. She thought
back to orienteering with Forest Club.
If she were standing in the middle of a
clock face facing south, the hut would
be at twelve o'clock and the town of
Winston would be in the direction of
two o'clock.

"Easy, we'll walk towards two o'clock!
Let's go!" Fliss said cheerily but when
she looked for Nanuk, he was sitting
very still. "What it is, Nanuk?" she
asked, her pulse racing. If it was another
wolf pack, they were in trouble.

Fliss followed the bear cub's intense
gaze across the snow. There, sitting
prettily in a shower of snowflakes, was

an Arctic fox.

The fox was the same size as Nanuk, with long fur and a bushy tail. It was totally white, apart from its black whiskers and little black pointy nose. Fliss stared too. It was beautiful and so delicate-looking. She didn't think the fox would be a threat to a little bear, although she knew she should check. It was always better to know the facts.

"Foxes sometimes follow polar bears to scavenge remains," she read. She looked up and saw the fox had turned and was walking away. Within seconds it would disappear from sight, camouflaged by the snow.

"If foxes follow polar bears, perhaps we should follow the fox. It might lead us to your mum. Come on, Nanuk!"

Trying to keep close without scaring it away, Fliss and Nanuk followed the fox. It was trotting so lightly it looked as if it was dancing.

With the snow deepening underfoot and the falling flakes in their eyes, it was getting harder and harder to keep up with the little fox.

Arctic hares didn't help either. They kept bouncing across the snow in front of them, startling Nanuk and making him fall over. And when he wasn't falling over, he wanted to play with them.

Polar bears, walruses, wolves, hares and foxes! I must have seen nearly all the North Pole animals! How lucky am I? Fliss thought.

They reached the top of a snow mound and saw the fox making its way down the other side. It was no longer trotting – it had started running. Fliss wiped the snow from her eyes, straining to keep the fox in sight.

"I think it's seen something. We need to hurry!"

Raiding the Bins

The fox was now out of sight but Fliss
was using her snowshoes to ski down
the slope, following the fox's tiny paw
prints. The snow was easing off and the
big cloud was moving, pushed on by a
strong wind that felt like ice daggers on
Fliss's cheeks.

She dug the sides of her shoes into
the snow and stopped. Nanuk, who was
rolling and tumbling behind, bumped
into her legs.

"Steady, Nanuk," Fliss said. "We need to be careful. Look."

In the distance, Fliss could make out a road. It had been snow-ploughed and looked like a black snake weaving in and out of the snowy fields below. On one side of the road were big bins – an out-of-town rubbish site. Some of the bins had been tipped over, their contents spread on the ground. There was movement and Fliss took a look through the binoculars.

A little cub was sniffing some rubbish and she could see a large white bottom poking out from between two bins.

"Could it be…?"

Nanuk hadn't seen his family because he was more interested in picking apart Fliss's snowshoes again. Fliss wondered what she should do. How would she get Nanuk to his mother without putting herself in danger? She couldn't just walk up to a grown polar bear. Fliss decided to watch them a while. If they started walking on, perhaps she could take a short cut in the same direction and place Nanuk in their path.

The mother bear shuffled backwards out from between the bins. She was big, fluffy and it looked like she was well fed. And between her legs a second cub was playing.

"Oh dear," Fliss sighed. "That's not your mum after all. It's another bear family."

She continued to look at the bin-raiders, feeling a heaviness in her heart. These bears should be out hunting for seals, not searching for scraps to eat in garbage left by humans. It was so wrong.

Fliss knew from documentaries she'd watched about climate change and melting sea ice that polar bears were finding it harder to hunt naturally. Seals popped their heads up through holes in the ice to breathe and that's when the bears caught them. But if there was no ice, there was no hunting platform for the bears... It looked as if this mother bear had got used to finding her food in rubbish tips.

If only I could point them in the direction of the sea, where the ice is still strong enough to hunt, thought Fliss. *If only I could make things go back to normal.*

As if the mother bear had read her thoughts, she stopped scratching and gave the air a good sniff.

That's right, smell the sea, Fliss willed. Then the mother bear stood on her two giant back legs, raising the front ones off the ground. She was so tall it took Fliss's breath away. The bear continued to sniff the air then stopped and stared in their direction.

"Uh-oh," Fliss muttered. "Nanuk, we have to go. Although you're gorgeous, I don't think this mum is pleased to see you. Or me..."

What Fliss didn't say is that rival bears could sometimes kill each other, even little cubs. And this one had their scent. What on Earth were they going to do? They couldn't outrun a grown bear. Fliss racked her brains, thinking of her Forest Club lessons. There was nothing about animal scents, they were about what to do as a human in a forest. They learned how to survive in the wild and how to do as little damage to the environment as possible by not overturning logs and rocks, taking home litter and covering up signs of ever being there.

Covering up... Maybe they could hide in the snow. No, polar bear noses were far too good for that. The animal book said they could smell a seal from twenty miles away! Hiding wasn't an option. Fliss grunted in frustration as she tried to think what to do. As if talking back to her, the mother bear gave a low growl in the distance. A look through the binoculars told Fliss she didn't have long. The mother bear and her cubs had started lumbering in their direction.

"I have to use what I know," Fliss said to herself. "It's what vets do every time they look at an injured animal..."

Fliss went back to the sense of smell. If they were interested in smell then that's what she and Nanuk should give them. A decoy scent, while they made their escape.

"Quickly, Nanuk," Fliss said,

unwinding the scarf from her neck.
"Have a good rub."

She ran the scarf under and over the
bear's body. Of course Nanuk thought it
was another game! She didn't have time
to play so Fliss picked up a snowball
and threw it back down the other side
of the hill for Nanuk to chase. Then
she took off her jacket and removed a
couple of shirt layers from underneath
before putting the jacket back on.

Fliss threw the bundle of clothes to
her right before skiing back down the
opposite side of the hill after Nanuk.
She had to hope that the bears would
find the clothes, head in the wrong
direction and then give up. If they
didn't, Fliss and Nanuk would be in
deep trouble.

"Come on, let's get back to the shore and follow it round to the hut as quickly as we can," Fliss urged as she caught up with the cub. "It's the only place we'll be safe."

10

Stampede

When they reached the shore, Fliss dared to look back through her binoculars. There was no sign of the big mother bear. Although she knew she couldn't exactly relax, Fliss figured it would be OK to stop and take a few big breaths.

With all the snow-trekking and excitement, she was tired. Nanuk also looked slower and wobblier on his feet. She watched him toying with the thin cracking ice at the edge of the bay and smiled. He was so young, curious and playful. But she couldn't look after him forever.

Fliss looked around the bay hoping to see bears out on the ice – still there was nothing. Only the walrus huddle in the distance. Then movement further along the shore caught her eye… A herd of something. What were they?

As they moved closer, she could see their chocolate-brown coats with the thick white bands around their necks and the growths on top of their heads. Some growths were little hard stumps, others were more fully formed – bony structures jutting upwards, with bumps on the sides.

"Caribou," Fliss gasped. "Just when

I thought I'd seen all the animals out here, there's more!"

She was so transfixed by the reindeer she didn't see Nanuk's reaction to the herd. He was off to investigate these large creatures! He ran forwards, startling them. They reversed and bucked as Nanuk wove between their legs.

"Nanuk, stop!" Fliss cried. But it was no good – he was having too much fun.

The caribou weren't impressed by the little cub and decided they were going to get out of the way. Nanuk shot out the back of the herd and turned to look at Fliss, who was staring at the reindeer. They had spread out in a line and were trotting towards her. As Nanuk chased

from the back, they started to stampede forwards. Fliss knew they didn't mean her any harm but if she got caught up in their charge, she'd be in trouble.

The caribou didn't seem to notice she was in their way and were picking up speed, their cantering hooves drumming and occasionally slipping on ice. In a few seconds they'd be on top of her.

There was nowhere left to go except the sea ice in the bay.

Fliss flung herself on to the ice in a penguin slide with such force she couldn't stop. She spread out her arms and legs and went into a starfish spin until she slowed down.

She lay still, catching her breath and listening to the fading caribou stampede, wondering how on Earth she had managed to find herself in charge of the naughtiest polar bear in the Arctic.

She felt a thud on her back, then a weight pressing down on her spine. A cub-size weight.

"Nanuk!" Fliss squeezed the words from her compressed chest. "You're supposed to be interesting in chasing seals, not reindeer ten times your size!"

Nanuk started patting the back of her head and her hair got tangled in his paws.

"Enough now," said Fliss, rolling over and tipping the cub on to the ice. "You must be the most fidgety little animal I've ever met!"

Fliss pushed Nanuk on one side, so he spun round on the ice.

"Now you know what it's like!" She laughed. Nanuk immediately came back for more.

Fliss spun him again and again, laughing until her tummy hurt. Then the cub crawled into her lap and curled up like a kitten. Sitting out on the ice with her snuggly friend, Fliss felt as if she was in a dream. The white landscape, the crisp air, the polar bear cuddles. It was magical. Fliss wished it could stay this way.

"So far we've met caribou, a fox, a pack of wolves, a few Arctic hares, some blubbery walruses and an unfriendly polar bear family. You've certainly taken me on an adventure, Nanuk. But I'm supposed to be taking *you* home!"

She raised her binoculars. After the encounter with the polar bears they hadn't gone towards two o'clock. Instead they'd gone towards the bay, at nine o'clock. And the lookout hut remained just a dot on the other side. Fliss felt her head spin and as soon as she stood, her muscles ached. There was still no sign of bears, although she couldn't trust her eyes any more. And without her under layers, she was starting to feel really cold. Cold to the bone.

Fliss knew she should probably get back to the safety of the hut as soon as possible. She had been on the move all day, walking and skiing in her funny shoes. Her energy was used up. She needed to rest and recharge.

There was bound to be an energy bar in the survival kit and if she burrowed out a snow den, she could keep warm. Especially with a fluffy polar bear to snuggle up to. She stroked Nanuk's coat.

"I-I-I'm not sure if I've got the energy to w-w-walk back to th-th-the hut," she said, teeth chattering. "H-how about we m-m-make a den and rest for a b-b-bit?"

As Fliss pulled herself back across the ice, her muscles shook and her body started to shiver. Her tired eyes danced with stars and Nanuk walked close to her as if he sensed she was exhausted.

"I'm fine, Nanuk," she said, forcing a big smile. But she wasn't sure if she was, or if she'd ever be able to reunite him with his family. And that thought was harder to bear than the freezing air that was nipping at her toes and fingers and numbing her skin.

Snug in the Snow

Fliss put every last drop of energy
into finding a safe resting place and
eventually headed for a large snowdrift
that had formed between two giant
rocks along the bay.

"All we need to do is burrow a hole in
that and crawl inside," Fliss explained to
the cub, who was staring up at the huge
mound of snow.

She took off her snowshoes and used
the wooden boards to help hollow

out an area at the bottom of the drift.
Nanuk helped by scratching away at the
surface. His company gave her strength.

"That's right, little one. We're a team!"

When she had made a rough cave, Fliss
crawled inside to dig further, smoothing
the walls with her palms as she went. She
had once seen a survival expert on
television do this. It was to stop little
peaks of snow that would then drip and
make you wet. The smoother it was, the
stronger it was. Her teeth were chattering
but she kept going. Nanuk had given up
and was leaning against her legs.

"Not long, Nanuk. Not long."

When the hole was deep enough that
it was dark, Fliss crawled inside and sat
at the end. She giggled when she saw his
face at the entrance peering in at her.

"Come inside, we'll soon be w-w-warm," she said. The cub trotted in and tried to curl up in her lap.

"W-wait, I need to do one m-more thing."

Fliss crawled back into the open. With some of the scooped-out snow, she made a large snowball and backed into the cave holding the snowball in front of her. It wedged tight inside the entrance, leaving a couple of small gaps that let in some light. This way they wouldn't draw attention from any more passing animals. It was dark now and she felt around in her backpack, fumbling for a torch. She turned it on to see Nanuk waiting patiently for her. As soon as she was settled, he jumped right back into her lap.

"I'm tired too," Fliss said. She needed energy but falling asleep in the cold wasn't a good idea – her heart would slow down too much.

In the survival kit she found some pouches of food. She tore off the corners and squirted them into her mouth. She didn't know what flavour they were or even recognize the taste. But they made her feel warmer.

She stroked Nanuk, who occasionally reached out a paw and patted her back.

On her adventures, Fliss had
experienced moments where she couldn't
believe how lucky she was. This was
definitely one of them! Adult polar bears
were ferocious loners and people rarely
got close. Yet here she was in a den in the
Arctic, cuddling up with a frost-white
polar bear cub. Nanuk stretched and
yawned then snuggled into Fliss's
tummy. The poor thing must be
exhausted – all that playing and walking,
with no nourishing milk…

Nanuk wasn't sleepy for long. He sat
up, alert.

Fliss could hear it too. A strange noise
outside the cave. A short rasping sound
– like a chuffing steam train. Fliss's
heart thumped. What was it?

Nanuk was on his feet, standing on

Fliss's thighs. He made a funny little roar.

"Let's go and take a look," Fliss said.

She nudged him off her lap and crawled to the entrance, where she broke away some of the snowball to make a peephole.

Nothing.

At least not immediately outside the den. Fliss made the hole larger to give her a wider view and there, out on the ice, was a large, thin polar bear, accompanied by one small, fluffy cub.

Feeling her heart swell and tears prickle at the corners of her eyes, Fliss retreated into the snow cave to get her binoculars. She had to be certain.

She pushed away more of the snowball and held up the binoculars. It was definitely Nanuk's mother and there was a little bit of red round her mouth. Blood! She had managed to find something to eat! Thank goodness. And the little cub? He was staring down at the ice. Fliss could make out a dark patch – an air hole. They were hunting seals! Fliss shuffled back and took Nanuk in her arms.

"You have to go now, little one, or you'll miss your hunting lesson!"

Nanuk was excited. He sensed his family was near and could hear his mother's call. He also seemed unwilling to leave Fliss. She felt the same, but she was here to reunite the cub with his mother and the time had come.

Fliss pushed Nanuk's fluffy bottom ahead of her so he was at the front of the snow tunnel. Reaching an arm forwards, she pushed the snowball so it rolled away from the entrance. The cub stopped and stared out at the ice, where his mother and sibling were waiting. He looked back at Fliss.

"No, I can't take you," she said with a lump in her throat. "You have to do this on your own."

Nanuk brushed his face against Fliss's cheek. Then he ran.

Fliss shuffled forwards into the mouth of the cave and sat and watched.

Her little cub made a funny clucking noise as he scooted back down the bank towards the ice. Happiness maybe, or hunger. Fliss watched closely through the binoculars. She didn't want to miss a second. She gasped as she saw Nanuk forget the change in surface and run on to the ice as if it were solid ground. He skidded across it on all fours, scrabbling the last few metres to get to his mother as quickly as possible.

Please accept him back, Fliss begged silently as she watched them face each other.

12

A Bear Hug

Mother and son gently touched noses and Fliss felt her cold body flood with warmth. The two cubs then touched noses before batting each other in the face with their giant paws. Fliss laughed out loud. She couldn't help it.

She felt sorry for the mother bear looking after two playful, naughty cubs. If Nanuk's sibling was anything like him, she was going to have her paws full!

The mother bear sat down on the ice

on her haunches and the cubs leaped on to her tummy to feed. Fliss watched this amazing display of wildlife and survival in front of her. She suddenly realized how off-guard she had become. The mother was looking right at her.

Uh-oh. A mother bear guarding two cubs... Fliss gulped. This was probably the most dangerous situation she had even been in. If there was an attack, she didn't have anything that could save her, and there was nowhere she could run to fast enough.

But the mother bear didn't rise up. After staring at Fliss for a few seconds she looked away. Perhaps she knew that Fliss had brought Nanuk back to her... It was a nice thought.

"I did bring him back," Fliss

whispered. "I wouldn't have given up until I did."

After feeding, the bears moved further out on the ice towards the open sea. One of the cubs stopped and turned a few times. Fliss waved but soon they were so far away she couldn't tell them apart from the rocky blocks of ice. They had disappeared from sight.

Fliss sighed, happy and sad all at once. She noticed the light was fading. It was time to go home. But how? Why hadn't she been transported the moment Nanuk had found his mother? Maybe she needed to get back to the hut to record the sighting and then her job would be done.

Fliss followed the shoreline south, to the other side of the bay where the lookout hut stood. Above her, the sky was rapidly darkening. The snow remained an eerie whitish-blue. She could make out the dark shapes of the boats moored up ahead.

"I hope they're boats," Fliss said to herself. "I wouldn't want to meet a walrus in the dark!"

The sky was deep indigo when she

finally reached the hut. The inside was
warm and smelled of wood fires, and
for a moment she thought of curling up
on the sofa. But Fliss wasn't ready to
sleep yet. She felt alive, tingling with the
excitement of what she'd achieved.

She filled out the *Polar Sightings* sheet
with as much information as she could,
smiling at how the next person to come
would scratch their heads, wondering
who had written it. Then Fliss went to
the bunk room and found a sleeping
bag. She took it outside and sat at the
end of the jetty, noticing at once a large
fluffy polar bear and two chubby cubs
out on the ice. The trash-can bears had
found their way to the proper hunting
grounds!

Fliss smiled and looked up at the

sky. The indigo had turned to black and stars had begun to appear, little twinkling confetti in the sky. Fliss had never seen so many stars. Millions, trillions even and … wow! Rippling bands of luminous green fluttered across the sky like a giant frilly skirt. Stripes and waves of blues and purples began to curl above them. The aurora borealis! Fliss had always dreamed of seeing the Northern Lights. Perhaps her journey had been extended just a little bit longer so she could witness this phenomenon.

Fliss watched the orchestra of light playing above her and thought of her friend Nanuk, who had brought so much colour to her life. She lay back on the jetty and closed her eyes so she could imagine his cheeky little face...

"What are you doing? We're supposed to be playing – not sleeping!" It was Ella's voice.

Fliss sat bolt upright, eyes wide in alarm. She was in a sleeping bag in her tent, the sun rippling on the canvas above her. She was back!

"Where have you been?" Ella insisted.

"Just enjoying the aurora borealis," Fliss said. "Come on, let's join the others."

"Found her, she's here!" Ella said triumphantly.

"You were the last one," Taylor said. "Were you in your tent the whole time? What a boring hiding place!"

"Yes, she was being a snory-bory alice."

All the children wrinkled their noses in confusion. Fliss laughed. "What's a snory-bory alice?"

"It's like a silly billy, or a smart alec, for someone who'd rather sleep than have fun. You should know, *you* said it!" Ella said, shaking her head as if Fliss was the silly one.

"Oh, the *aurora borealis*!" Fliss
laughed. "The Northern Lights, Ella."

Ella slapped her hand to her mouth
and spluttered with giggles. No one
thought to ask Fliss why she was
watching the aurora borealis in her tent,
and luckily Karen and Andrew arrived
before anyone could.

"We're still not quite ready for a
campfire, kids, so are there any ideas for
another quick game?"

"How about a treasure hunt?" Fliss
suggested. "We could collect litter?"

"That's not treasure!" Pippa moaned.
"It's rubbish."

"We treasure our wildlife, don't we?
If animals eat the litter we leave it
might hurt them. Besides, it's definitely
treasure if we get extra marshmallows

115

for being good citizens." Fliss looked at the camp leaders pleadingly.

They nodded and there was a big cheer.

"Come on, Fliss," Ella said, grabbing her hand and pulling her towards the woods. "Let's pick the most litter and get loads of marshmallows!"

They ran between the trees, eyes peeled for glinting wrappers.

Then there was a shout – Taylor
had found some rubbish! – and Ella
ran off to see. But Fliss stopped. She
had spotted tracks in the muddy forest
floor! Large oval prints, each with five
claw marks along the top. She
recognized the shape, although
she'd only ever seen them in
the snow, not mud.

Fliss followed the prints
deep into the forest where
they stopped suddenly at a
large tree covered in thick
bark.

At first Fliss saw only the
large cramp ball in the middle of the
trunk – a roundish black nub – but
when she stood back, she gasped. There
was a pattern in the bark. The cramp

ball was a nose, and the rest… It was unmistakable. A face of a polar bear!

"Nanuk!" Fliss wrapped her arms around the tree. It felt softer than bark should, as if the tree were hugging her right back.

She would have stayed there forever, if it weren't for her name being called over and over. It was campfire time.

"I've got to go." She stood back. Was it her imagination or did the little bear smile? "Bye bye, Nanuk. I'll never forget you," Fliss said, as the image melted into the bark. Beneath her feet, the paw prints slowly vanished into the mud.

Back at camp, Ella was sitting by the fire singing, "Let's all yell-o for a squidgy marshmallow!" loudly. She stopped when she saw Fliss. "What are those white marks on your fleece? It looks like you've been hugged by a snow monster!"

Fliss looked down to see her top was covered in ice crystals! "Perhaps I have," she said, seeing the last sparkles of Nanuk's hug melt away. "Or perhaps I was hugged by a playful snowy polar bear."

"In your dreams, Fliss!" Pippa snorted.

Fliss's eyes twinkled brightly as her friends laughed around the campfire and she watched the sparks dance up into the sky.

Rachel Delahaye was born in Australia but has
lived in the UK since she was six years old. She
studied linguistics and worked as a magazine writer
and editor before becoming a children's author. She
loves words and animals; when she can combine the
two, she is very happy indeed! At home, Rachel loves
to read, write and watch wildlife documentaries.
Outside, she loves to go walking in woodland.
She also follows news about animal rights and the
environment and hopes that one day the world will
be a better home for all species, not just humans!

Rachel has two lively children and a dog called
Rocket, and lives in the beautiful city of Bath.